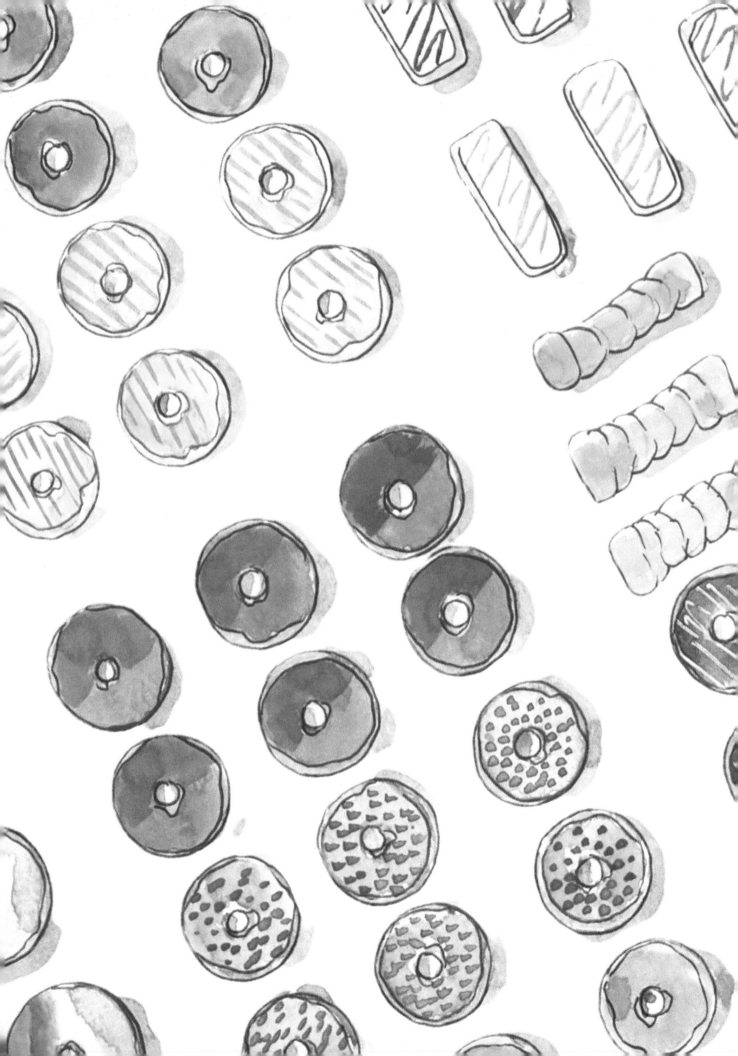

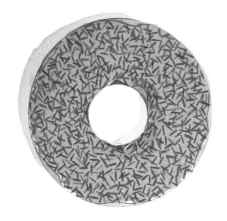

First edition, June 2022

Printed by IngramSpark

ISBN 978-0-578-36736-1 (hardcover)

ISBN 979-8-218-01190-1 (paperback)

Sprinkles

Written by Allison Wood

Illustrated by Samuel Waddle

LIFE IS SHORT... BE MESSY!

For The Herd and My Team

~A.W.

To Sara, Badgley and Suri

~S.W.

Julia's dad stood between piles of books and boxes while Luna circled his legs, meowing for her breakfast. "Julia, where are you?" Julia burst out of a giant moving box. "There is a bakery nearby. Let's get some breakfast before Grandma visits. It's a beautiful morning for a walk." Julia grabbed her sweater while dad heaped food into Luna's dish.

Julia enjoyed walking, skipping, and hopping the four blocks to the bakery. Her one hand squeezed Dad's hand while her other hand waved at all of the interesting people and pets that filled the streets.

The bakery was warm and filled with delicious smells. Dad ordered coffee and told Julia she could choose a doughnut.

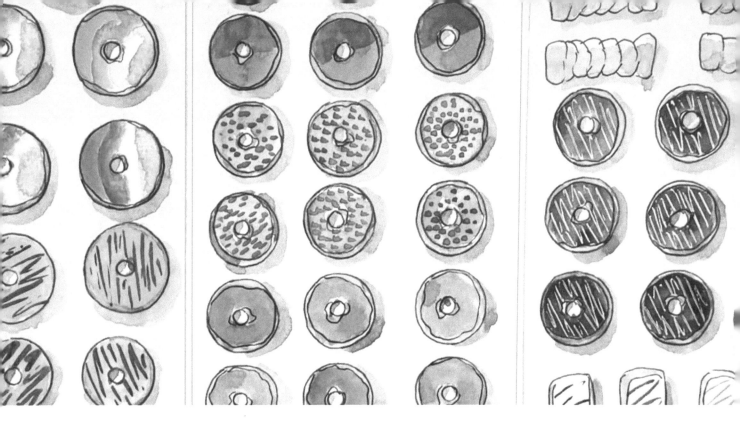

Julia's eyes widened, and her mouth watered as she peered through the glass bakery case.

There were circle doughnuts, ring doughnuts, and rectangle doughnuts. There were lumpy, bumpy, twisty, and swirly doughnuts. There were chocolate doughnuts, vanilla doughnuts, and doughnuts oozing with jam, custard, and cream. There were doughnuts covered with coconut, honey, caramel, nuts, fruit, and even bacon! There were boring plain doughnuts too. "Who eats those?" Julia wondered.

Julia's eyes settled on the best doughnut in the case.

"I want the pretty, pink, super-sprinkly doughnut, please," she said happily to the baker.

She kept a watchful eye on the sweet treat. The baker smiled as he carefully put her doughnut into a bag.

Now, Julia held tight to both the bakery bag and Dad's hand. They walked, skipped, and hopped the four blocks back home, and Julia was happy to see some kids her age in their new neighborhood.

"I'm going to unpack a few more boxes before Grandma gets here," Dad said as Julia carefully took her pretty, pink, super-sprinkly doughnut out of its bag.

It was almost too pretty to eat. Almost. Julia took a giant bite and licked her lips. It was delicious!

Sprinkles tumbled off of the doughnut and onto the counter and floor. Sprinkles dashed off of the doughnut and onto the boxes. Sprinkles jumped onto Luna, who shook wildly to free the sugary bits from her fur.

The sprinkles flew everywhere! Rainbow sprinkles dove into the fishbowl, and Bubble's eyes grew wide.

Julia continued eating while Luna batted sprinkles across the smooth floor with her paws. The sprinkles danced from the kitchen to the living room.

After a few more bites, the doughnut was gone. Sprinkles bounced off of Julia's sweater and out of her hair.

Julia looked at their new kitchen, its shiny floors and counters now dotted in rainbow sprinkles.

Sprinkles decorated the piles of moving boxes. It was a fantastic sight, but Julia knew the mess must be cleaned before Grandma's visit.

She began picking the sprinkles up one by one, but it seemed like for each one she captured, four more appeared.

Julia tried to push the sprinkles into neat piles but the sprinkles had a mind of their own, twisting and twirling every which way.

Julia thought for sure she saw sprinkles winking at her as she tried to clean the mess. She dug through some boxes and found a dustpan and broom and started chasing the sprinkles around the kitchen.

Luna used her tail like a mop and pushed sprinkles into piles. The more they cleaned, the farther and faster the sprinkles spread.

Julia needed something more powerful to contain them.
"Dad, where is the vacuum cleaner?" Dad appeared in the
kitchen. "Why do you need the—Oh!" His eyes grew wide and
his face turned a little red, but he laughed.

"Did any sprinkles make it into your tummy? I'm proud of you
for starting to clean up, and I can help you finish. These
sprinkles are no match for the vacuum cleaner."

The vacuum was hungry and gobbled up sprinkles from the floor. Dad used the plastic hose like a straw to suck up sprinkles from the corners and tight spaces. He attached a brush, and the vacuum inhaled the little sprinkle mountains Julia and Luna created.

Julia used a spoon to carefully scoop the swimming sprinkles out of the fishbowl.

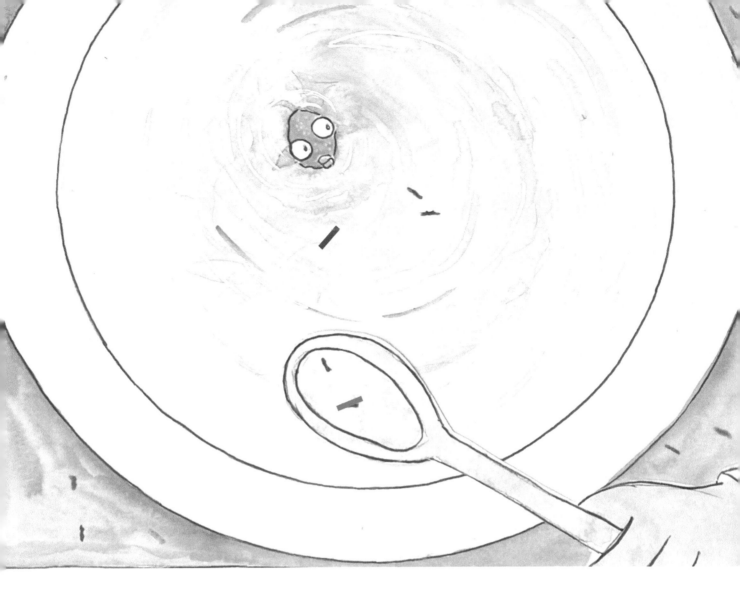

DING...
DING...

Dad quickly put the vacuum, broom, and dustpan into the closet as Julia ate a lone red sprinkle off of her sweater.

"Grandma!" Julia jumped into Grandma's arms for a warm hug. Then, she proudly showed off the new apartment. "It's so bright and clean," Grandma commented, and Dad winked at Julia.

Grandma helped unpack the kitchen boxes, and there was almost no sign of the morning's sprinkle mess.

"I stopped at a lovely bakery on my way here and picked out a treat for us," said Grandma. She scooped up the white box that Luna was sniffing by the door.

Julia's eyes grew wide, and Dad laughed softly as Grandma opened the box.

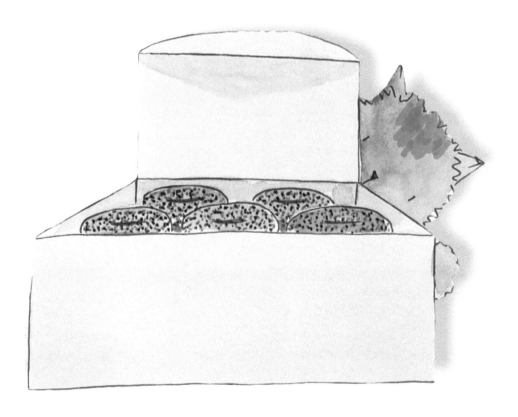

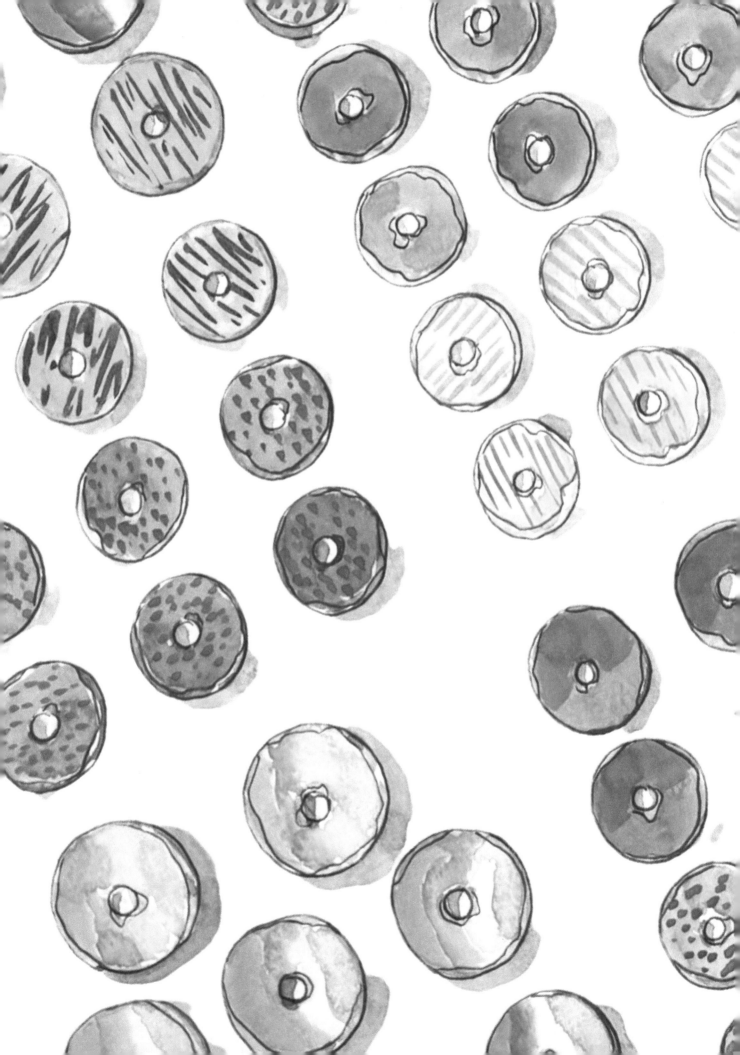

CPSIA information can be obtained
at www.ICGtesting.com
Printed in the USA
BVHW022153100722
641814BV00002B/10